Illustration by: Branillius
Book cover title design by: Xee Shan
Editor: Kristin Cebulski

ISBN: 979-8-9894752-1-6 (Paperback)

OCYRUS INK PUBLISHING

JOHN
SAVES
CHRISTMAS

BY
O'CYRUS

ILLUSTRATED BY
BRANILLIUS

So, there I was sitting by my fireplace, drinking hot chocolate wondering what Santa Claus would bring me for Christmas. I had been on my best behavior throughout the year so, I decided to write him a letter and mail it to the North Pole.

Dear Santa Claus,

I was wondering if I could have some really cool toys, video games, and a bicycle this year. I promise to leave you a glass of milk and a bowl filled with chocolate chip cookies. I know that's your favorite. Oh, and Santa . . . I have one more present to ask for. I know it may sound silly, but could you please give me friends? It's just that—I don't have a brother or sister and it gets really lonely. I just wish I had friends to spend time with. Thank you Santa Claus.

Sincerely,
John

I dressed myself then headed outside
to drop my letter into the mailbox.

I was so excited I could hardly lay still in bed, but soon I was able to sleep. However, while I was asleep I was awakened to a loud knock at my front door—

"Good evening John. My name is Sebastian, and this is my brother Noah. We traveled from the North Pole to ask for your help. You see—Santa Claus received your letter, but there is a big problem; he is terribly sick and will be unable to deliver gifts this Christmas unless we do something fast! Can you please come with us back to our village to help?"

Without hesitation I ran outside
and followed them to their sleigh.

Within minutes we arrived at the North Pole, dropped off their sleigh, and we rushed over to Santa's home by foot.

We soon arrived at his home and Mrs. Claus kindly opened the front door to speak with us.

She explained how Santa wasn't feeling well and Christmas was on the verge of being canceled unless we could find medicine to help him recover by midnight. Unfortunately, Mrs. Claus couldn't accompany us as she did not want to leave Santa unattended, so it was up to us to find the cure for him. Mrs. Claus recommended we search his office in the workshop back in the village for answers.

With only five hours left until Christmas we left Santa's home, returned back to the village, and entered his office in the workshop.

We searched everywhere but couldn't find anything helpful. That was until I realized something . . .

"Milk and cookies! We need milk and cookies!" I shouted. I asked if they knew where we could obtain the best milk and cookies on the planet and Sebastian mentioned a small city known as Eutopia. A lady named Mrs. Castillo was known for her top notch baking skills and is always willing to help.

So . . . We hoped onto their sleigh and headed towards Eutopia.

We arrived at Mrs. Castillo's home and knocked on her front door until she answered. We explained the condition Santa was in and asked if she wouldn't mind providing us with her magical milk and cookies as we were certain this would help Santa recover.

She nodded with a smile and yelled for her son, Abel Jr, to grab a pack of freshly baked cookies from their pantry and a carton of Eutopian whole-milk from their refrigerator.

Abel Jr ran towards his mother who directs him to present the milk and cookies to John.

The end of Christmas eve was fast approaching, so we left Eutopia and headed directly towards Santa's home to deliver the goods to Mrs. Claus.

Sebastian and Noah needed to finish wrapping the children's Christmas gifts, so they dropped me off at Santa's doorstep and headed back to the workshop.

"Oh, this is perfect!" Mrs. Claus cheered.

She thanked me, took the milk and cookies, and asked that I take a seat in the living room to wait for her.

Several minutes later Mrs. Claus and I exited her home to return to the village. While we were traveling she delivered some unexpected news . . . "Thank you so much for your help, John," said Mrs. Claus. "Santa was most grateful for your assistance and is recovering right now. Unfortunately, he has to rest through the night and will not be able to deliver gifts for Christmas this year . . . I am so sorry."

"This can't be real," I thought. "Santa Claus was invincible—how could an illness slow him down? Now children around the world will wake up to nothing this Christmas . . . I must do something!"

After Mrs. Claus reunited me with Sebastian and Noah I explained to them in secret what happened and devised a plan to save Christmas. We hurried towards their sleigh and traveled to Santa's home as quickly as possible before Mrs. Claus could learn anything.

Moments later a loud "GONG" sound echoed throughout the North Pole indicating midnight arrived and Christmas had officially begun.

We arrived at his home and snuck into an area where his sleigh and reindeer resided. I hopped onto his sleigh and tried to learn how to maneuver it. Meanwhile, Sebastian and Noah left the area to make sure the coast was clear.

Minutes later the sound of the door creaked open behind me.

"Such bravery you have John—I'd like to take-over from here if that's okay."

"The boys ran off to the village, but before they departed Noah mentioned this plan to save Christmas was your idea. How thoughtful and wise beyond your years you are. As a token of my gratitude, I will return you to your home safely in Casa Court."

Santa boarded the sleigh with me and within seconds we soared high into the sky and never looked back . . . We left so abruptly I didn't have a chance to say goodbye to Sebastian and Noah.

They were like the friends I never had but always wanted.

"Thank you Santa for bringing me back home," I said.

"You're quite welcome, John," Santa replied. "I have a long night ahead of me, so please forgive me if I seem rude, but I must get going now."

As Santa was leaving I quickly stopped him.

"Santa—I was wondering if you remembered what I wrote on my Christmas list?"

"John . . . I never forget what is on a Christmas list," Santa replied. "Go head inside to get some rest; when you awake, your gifts will be waiting for you."

"Thank you for everything Santa!"

"The pleasure is all mine, John . . . Take care young man!"

"HO HO HO!!! MERRY CHRISTMAS!!"

From that moment on Santa journeyed across the world and delivered gifts to children everywhere.

Santa Claus was cured, the children around the world received their gifts, and Christmas was saved.

So—I bet you're wondering if Santa delivered the gifts I asked for in the letter I mailed right?

Sebastian and Noah visited me later that day and promised they would come to my home and visit as often as possible.

Ultimately, the same two boys who pleaded for my help that night to save Santa ended up becoming my best friends.

So, children do well in school, be kind to others, and most importantly listen to your parents. If you do those things, I promise you Santa Claus will make sure you have the greatest Christmas ever.

For those reading or listening, please, have a very Merry Christmas and a happy new year!!

See you next time!